To my old pal Anders

Copyright © 2022 by Troy Cummings

All rights reserved. Published in the United States by Random House Children's Books,
a division of Penguin Random House LLC, New York.

Random House and the colophon are registered trademarks of Penguin Random House LLC.

Visit us on the Web! rhcbooks.com

Educators and librarians, for a variety of teaching tools, visit us at RHTeachersLibrarians.com

Library of Congress Cataloging-in-Publication Data is available upon request.
ISBN 978-0-593-43216-7 (trade) — ISBN 978-0-593-43217-4 (lib. bdg.) — ISBN 978-0-593-43218-1 (ebook)

MANUFACTURED IN CHINA
10 9 8 7 6 5 4 3 2 1
First Edition

IS THIS YOUR CLASS PET?

Troy Cummings

Random House 🏠 New York

DEAR PEOPLE AT SCHOOL,

WOOF!!!

THANK YOU FOR GIVING ME A JOB.

I WILL BE THE BEST HELPER DOG IN THE WHOLE LIBRARY:

MY SOFT FUR IS GOOD FOR CUDDLES.

MY EARS ARE GOOD FOR LISTENING TO STORIES.

AND I HARDLY EVER DROOL! (EXCEPT AT LUNCH TIME.)

YOUR HARD WORKER,

 ARFY

AUTHOR

TITLE

BORROWER'S NAME

DATE DUE

Thanks for your help today, Arfy! You look so dapper in your vest!

The children loved reading to you in the library. And it was so kind of you to stop by the cafeteria, the gym, the art room, and Mrs. Tortuga's class!

Whooooo's a good helper? You are!

-Ruby Saddlestitch

Librarian

- Send
- Fetch
- Speak
- Mark as read
- Mark as sniffed

TO: principal@butternut_elementary.edu

FROM: arfy@mail.dog

DEAR SCHOOL PRINCIPAL,

I AM GOOD AT FETCHING.
I FETCH STICKS.
I FETCH SQUEAKY TOYS.
ONE TIME I EVEN FETCHED UNDERPANTS.

BUT TODAY AT SCHOOL I FETCHED SOMETHING
BY ACCIDENT: A TEENY GREEN ROCK HIDING IN
MY VEST.

BUT IT WASN'T A ROCK! IT WAS A
TURTLE. SHE IS SHY AND QUIET BUT
ALSO BRAVE. I CALL HER HIDEY.

I THINK SHE MIGHT BE A CLASS PET!
WHAT SHOULD I DO?

ARFY

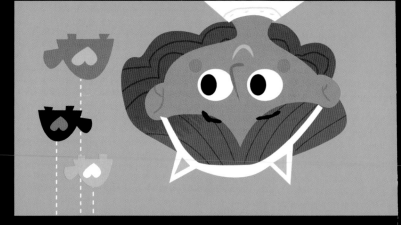

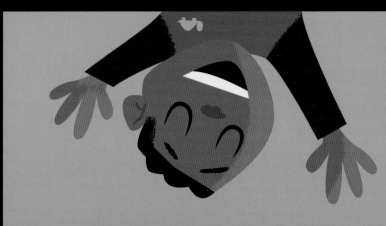

Arfy: YAY!

Mrs. Tortuga: Thank you, Arfy!

Isabel: We're so glad you found our pet!

Omar: She's so good at hiding!

Arfy: I KNOW! I CALL HER HIDEY! H.O.L. (HOWLING OUT LOUD)

Anna: Our class has been building a habitat for her.

Charlie: I have a pet snake at home and I love popcorn and my pants are blue!

Mrs. Tortuga: Arfy, could you bring Hidey back to us tomorrow?

Arfy: YEP!

Arfy: I MEAN, YES!

Arfy: OOPS, I SLOBBERED ON THE KEYBOARD. I'M SO EXCITED!

Arfy: W.M.T.O. (WAGGING MY TAIL OFF)

HOORAY!
YOU FOUND OUR TURTLE!

TAP TAP TAP

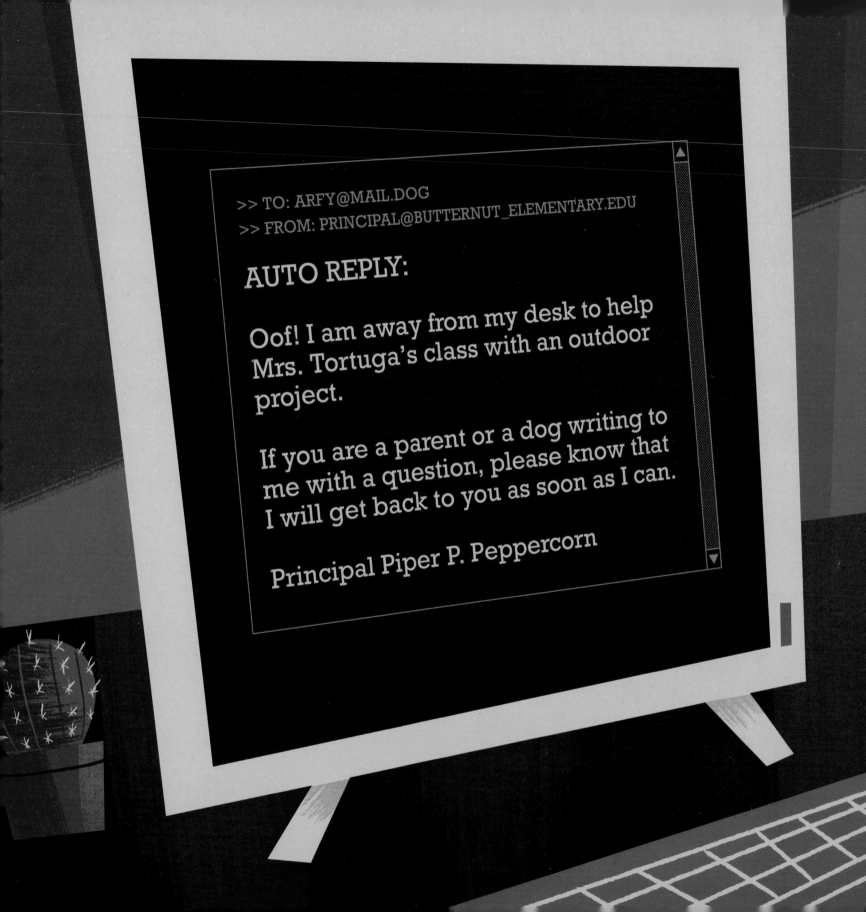

>> TO: ARFY@MAIL.DOG
>> FROM: PRINCIPAL@BUTTERNUT_ELEMENTARY.EDU

AUTO REPLY:

Oof! I am away from my desk to help
Mrs. Tortuga's class with an outdoor
project.

If you are a parent or a dog writing to
me with a question, please know that
I will get back to you as soon as I can.

Principal Piper P. Peppercorn

DEAR LUNCHROOM COOKS,

I FOUND A HUNGRY LITTLE TURTLE
WHO I CALL HIDEY.

SHE LOVES TO EAT PEAS AND
CARROTS AND LETTUCE AND APPLES
AND GRAPES.

AND THEN I REMEMBERED: YOU'VE
GOT PEAS AND CARROTS AND
LETTUCE AND APPLES AND GRAPES
IN THE CAFETERIA!

HIDEY MUST BE YOUR PET!

 ARFY

HIDEY

Hiya, doggo,

You know what else turtles eat? Bugs! And worms!

We're proud to say we NEVER have bugs and worms in our cafeteria. (No matter what you might hear from Mrs. Tortuga's class.)

Anyhoo, sorry to hear our little green friend is in such a pickle.

JEFF AND STEPH
the grade school chefs

P.S. You should always wash your hands—or paws!—when you've touched a turtle! And before eating or preparing food!

DEAR GYM COACH,

ARE YOU MISSING A TEENY-TINY TURTLE NAMED HIDEY?

 SHE CAN SIT.

 AND STAY.

 AND ALLLMOST ROLL OVER!

SHE'S ALSO AN EXPERT CLIMBER.

I FIGURED THE GYM IS THE PERFECT PLACE FOR ALL THAT FUN EXERCISEY STUFF!

 ARFY

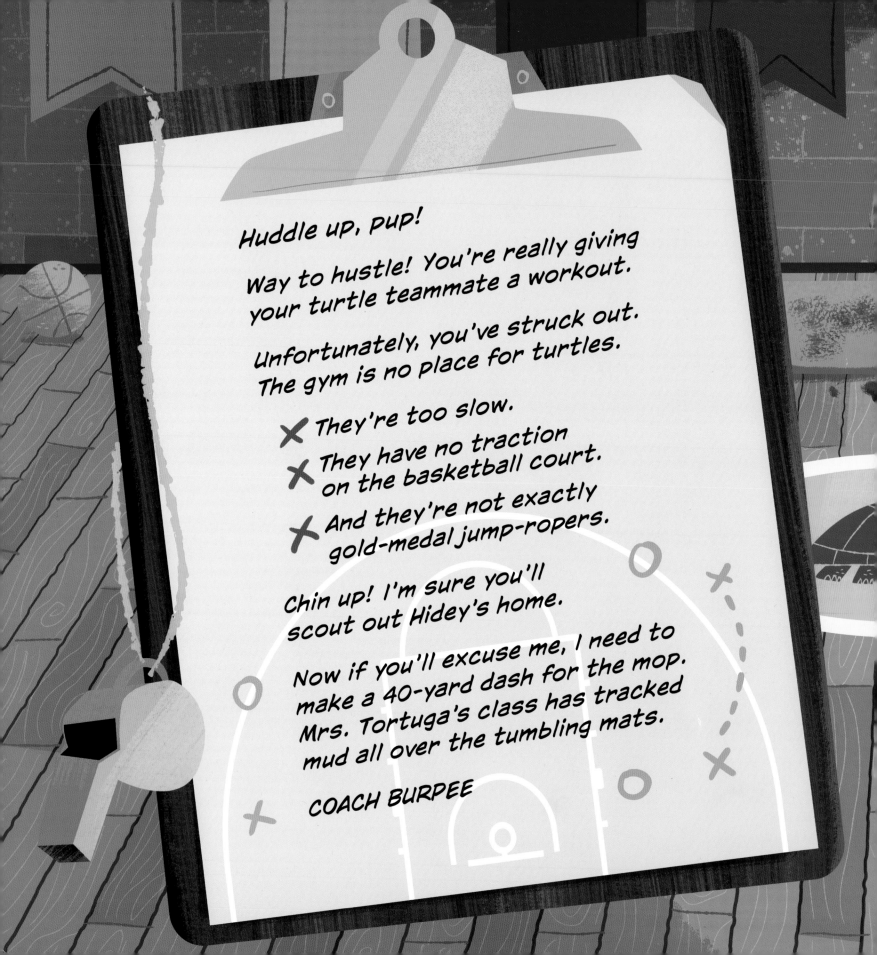

Huddle up, pup!

Way to hustle! You're really giving your turtle teammate a workout.

Unfortunately, you've struck out. The gym is no place for turtles.

✗ They're too slow.

✗ They have no traction on the basketball court.

✗ And they're not exactly gold-medal jump-ropers.

Chin up! I'm sure you'll scout out Hidey's home.

Now if you'll excuse me, I need to make a 40-yard dash for the mop. Mrs. Tortuga's class has tracked mud all over the tumbling mats.

COACH BURPEE

DEAR ART TEACHER,

I FOUND A TURTLE—AND I'M
PRETTY SURE SHE'S AN ARTIST!

SHE LIKES TO WORK IN SAND.
AND WATER. AND BITS OF
CHEWED-UP FOOD.

HER SHELL IS COVERED IN
BE-YOOO-TIFUL PATTERNS!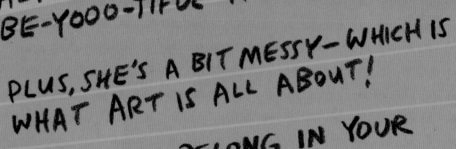

PLUS, SHE'S A BIT MESSY—WHICH IS
WHAT ART IS ALL ABOUT!

DOES SHE BELONG IN YOUR
ART ROOM?

YOUR PAL,

 ARFY

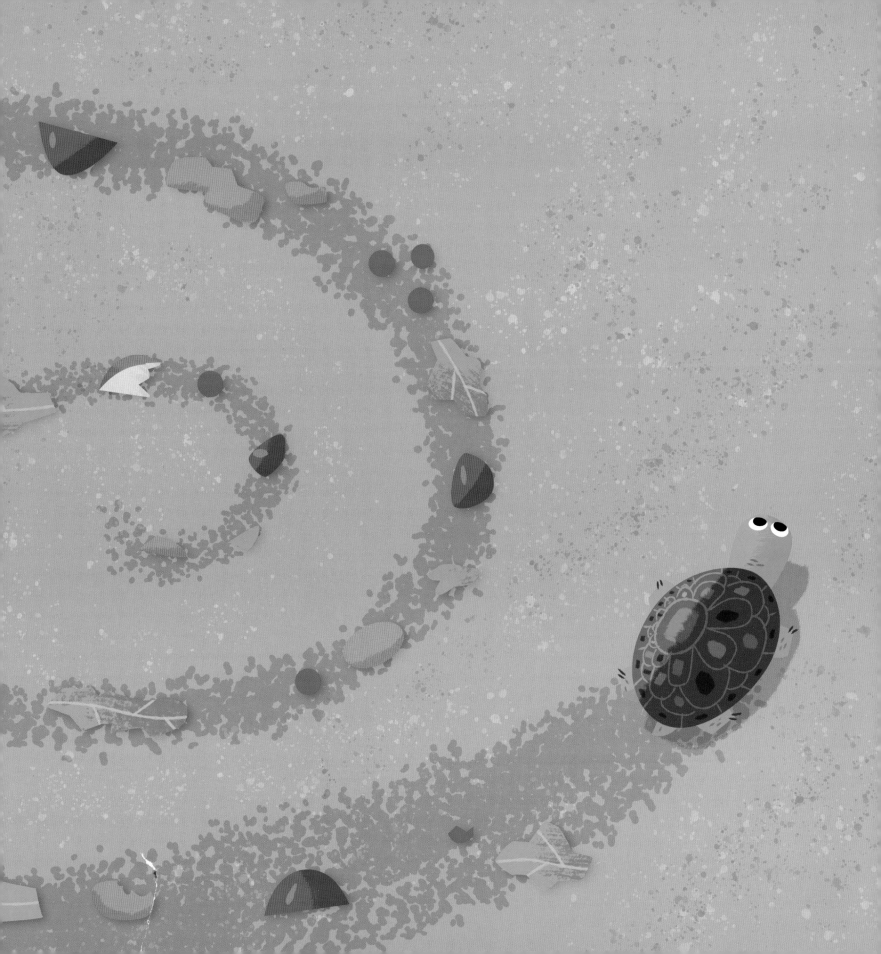

Oh, sweet Arfy!

We LOVE turtles! Our room is FULL of turtles! But ours are all works of art. (Just look at these pieces that Mrs. Tortuga's class just finished. Magnificent!)

I know you've been asking the grown-ups in our school about turtles, but maybe you should try asking the real experts!

Your pen pal
(and crayon pal
and brush pal!),

Dotty Stippler

Wiggle
Wiggle

"To protect your health, the earth and the animals,
please don't get a turtle for a pet!"
—The Humane Society

Turtles may seem like the perfect pet. They're beautiful. They're active. They're fun to study and draw. But turtles require years of special care.

*Turtles can transmit an infection called Salmonellosis. Wash your hands thoroughly after being around turtles.

*Turtles are not low-maintenance animals! They need the right lighting, temperature, and water, with plenty of space to climb and dig. They can live lonnnnng lives—some up to fifty years!

*You might be better off getting a cuddly stuffed turtle for your home and visiting real turtles at a zoo, animal rescue, or classroom.

*Learn more about how you can help turtles:

- humanesociety.org/news/thinking-getting-pet-turtle
- wcs.org/our-work/wildlife/tortoises-freshwater-turtles
- turtleconservancy.org

With love,

Mitzy

(Arfy's person)

P.S. If you're looking to adopt a kitty or doggo, please visit:
- theshelterpetproject.org
- bestfriends.org